GIRLS SURVIVE

Published by Stone Arch Books, an imprint of Capstone.
1710 Roe Crest Drive, North Mankato, Minnesota 56003
capstonepub.com

Library of Congress Cataloging-in-Publication Data

Names: Gilbert, Julie, 1976– author. | Wei, Wendy Tan Shiau, illustrator.
Title: Maddy and the monstrous storm : a Schoolhouse Blizzard survival story /
by Julie Gilbert ; illustrated by Wendy Tan. Other titles: Girls survive.
Description: North Mankato, Minnesota : Stone Arch Books, [2022] | Series: Girls
survive | Audience: Ages 8–12. | Audience: Grades 4–6. | Summary: Thirteen-
year-old Maddy struggles with prairie life on her aunt and uncle's farm in Dakota
Territory. But on January 12, 1888, when a blizzard threatens to trap Maddy and her
classmates inside their damaged schoolhouse, she finds the courage and strength to
lead them to safety. Includes historical note, glossary, and discussion questions.
Identifiers: LCCN 2021050690 (print) | LCCN 2021050691 (ebook) |
ISBN 9781666340686 (hardcover) | ISBN 9781666340723 (paperback) |
ISBN 9781666340730 (pdf)
Subjects: LCSH: Blizzards—Dakota Territory—History—19th century—Juvenile
fiction. | Norwegian Americans—Juvenile fiction. | Survival—Juvenile fiction. |
Courage—Juvenile fiction. | Aunts—Juvenile fiction. | Dakota Territory—History—
19th century—Juvenile fiction. | CYAC: Blizzards—Fiction. | Dakota Territory—
History—19th century—Fiction. | Survival—Fiction. | Norwegian Americans—
Fiction. | Courage—Fiction. | LCGFT: Historical fiction.
Classification: LCC PZ7.1.G549 Mad 2022 (print) | LCC PZ7.1.G549 (ebook) |
DDC 813.6 [Fic]—dc23/eng/20220110
LC record available at https://lccn.loc.gov/2021050690
LC ebook record available at https://lccn.loc.gov/2021050691

Editorial Credits
Editor: Alison Deering; Designer: Sarah Bennett;
Production Specialist: Katy LaVigne

Design Elements
Shutterstock: Max Lashcheuski (background texture),
Olena Rodina (snowflake background)

# MADDY AND THE MONSTROUS STORM

## A Schoolhouse Blizzard Survival Story

by Julie Gilbert

illustrated by Wendy Tan

STONE ARCH BOOKS
a capstone imprint

# CHAPTER ONE

Dakota Territory, near Aberdeen
Rolvig cabin
January 12, 1888
8:30 a.m.

"We're going to have to cut it off," Aunt Marta huffed. She wrestled a brush through my thick hair.

"Can't you just let it hang loose?" I asked, my voice a squeak. Aunt Marta was pulling so tightly that it brought tears to my eyes. "That's how I used to wear it at home."

Thinking of home—back in St. Paul, Minnesota—nearly brought more tears to my eyes. For the past five months, I had lived with Aunt Marta and Uncle Hans in Dakota Territory. I missed home desperately, even though *home* was no longer home.

Ever since my father had sent me here to live with his brother's family, I had struggled with farm life. I dropped the buckets of water I dragged from the well. I burned the bread. I cut my hands twisting hay into knots we would burn for fuel.

I couldn't sew, I couldn't cook, and I didn't know how to take care of children. Every time I picked up the baby, he cried. My cousin Cecelia was better at everything, and she was only seven.

"No," Aunt Marta said curtly, yanking me back to the present with another firm tug on my hair. "You'd end up getting it caught in the well rope. Or catching the ends on fire on the stove."

"That's not true," I mumbled under my breath, quietly enough that Aunt Marta wouldn't hear. But she had a point.

"Hurry up and grab your lunch and your books," Aunt Marta said once she'd finished with my hair. "You'll be late for school."

"Isn't Cecelia coming today?" I asked as Aunt Marta hurried me to the door. My cousin was at the table, mixing flour and water in a bowl.

"Cecelia's needed here," Aunt Marta said. "It's mild today, and we can catch up on chores. Uncle Hans and the older boys have been tending the cattle for hours already. We need to be efficient today."

I understood what she was really saying—I wasn't wanted here. I would only get in the way.

Behind Aunt Marta's back, Cecelia stuck out her tongue at me. Of all the Rolvigs, Cecelia resented my presence the most. As the only girl in a family of six, she worried I would take her place. At thirteen, I was almost twice as old as she was.

But Cecelia didn't have anything to worry about. She could run the household if necessary. I was too scared to touch the cows, much less milk them.

I opened the door of the tiny cabin. A soft breeze danced across my face and ruffled my skirt.

It had been below zero for the past two weeks, so the springlike warmth surprised me. Winters on the prairie were brutal. My cousins had told me horror stories of blizzards that lasted for days. Trains stopped running, and no one could leave the house because it was too cold.

"It's nice outside," I said, startled.

Aunt Marta rolled her eyes. "I told you that already. But take your warm cloak and mittens in case the weather turns."

"I don't need my cloak. It's like spring!" I exclaimed, stepping out the door and straight into the muddy farmyard. I twirled under the warm sun.

Aunt Marta shoved my cloak into my arms, along with my lunch pail. "Do as I say. And get going." With that, she turned and closed the door behind her.

I paused for a moment, staring at the cabin. It was tiny but made of wood, making it one of the nicest houses in the settlement. Many of the other farmers lived in one-room structures made of packed-dirt walls.

For a moment, I let myself remember my house in St. Paul. Father had sold it after the newspaper he ran went bankrupt. I still remembered the parlor full of books, though. And the bright kitchen where our housekeeper cooked delicious food.

I stood in the yard, blinking back tears. My mother had died when I was born, so it had always just been my father and me. Now it was just me.

Father was in Boston looking for work. He'd promised to send for me when he was settled. But that could be ages away.

In the meantime, I was stuck here. I had studied the Dakota Territory in our atlas when my father had told me where he was sending me. It was a wide stretch of land to the west of Minnesota. It wasn't even a state! Yet here I was, half a continent away from my father, living with strangers.

I had never met Uncle Hans, Aunt Marta, or any of their children before I'd stepped off the train. Uncle Hans had picked me up in a wagon pulled by two enormous draft horses. He'd barely said two words to me on the eight-mile drive from town to the farm. I'd never felt as alone or scared as I had sitting silently in the wagon as it bounced over the rough path.

A gentle breeze teased a few of my curls loose, and I shoved thoughts of home aside. There was no use crying over spilled milk, as Aunt Marta always said.

I started my walk across the prairie to school, picking my way over melting snowdrifts. It was a path I knew by heart. The route took me past the line of tiny fruit trees Uncle Hans had planted and across an open section of grassland to a small rise. A single massive cedar tree stood on top of the hill. The school sat at the bottom on the other side.

The walk normally took me ten minutes, but I dawdled, enjoying the fresh air. It was such a nice change from the freezing cold of the past weeks. The vast sky arched overhead, and I could see for miles in all directions.

There was so much space on the prairie. The view never changed. There was nothing but grassland in all directions, broken occasionally by tiny farms.

In the city, I felt at home. The big, crowded buildings and constant noise soothed me. Being out here made me feel small and insignificant. But at least I didn't have to listen to Aunt Marta's criticism for an entire day.

The relief I felt at being out of the house vanished when I reached the cedar at the top of the rise. The small, wooden schoolhouse was nestled into the prairie at the bottom of the hill. It contained a single room where everyone sat together, regardless of our grade. It couldn't have been more different from my school back in St. Paul—a massive brick building with twenty-seven rooms and almost three hundred students.

Shouts and laughter rose from the yard. There were seven of us today, including me. Two little kids were playing Fox and Geese on the far side of the building. On the closer side of the building, Ole Nilsen, Johann Gundersen, and Anna Dahl tossed a ball near the well.

*Maybe today they'll ask me to join them,* I thought.

Ole was fifteen while Johann and Anna were my age, but as usual, they ignored me. We were supposed to speak English at school, but Ole and the others usually spoke Norwegian when I walked past. Then they'd stare at me and laugh.

I was Norwegian too, but I couldn't understand what they said. My father had spoken English with

me. He was always telling me it was progress to cast off the customs of the old country.

Jane Berg was waiting for me on the steps. She was ten and had been born with one leg longer than the other. A special boot with a lift for her shorter leg made things a bit easier, but Jane still walked with a slight limp. It made it hard for her to play tag. Since no one let me play tag, we ended up sitting together most days.

"It's too warm today," Jane complained when I joined her.

"Johann, go back farther!" Ole shouted. He flung the ball through the air to Johann. I flinched as it sailed near us.

"I think it's nice," I replied, taking a breath to calm my nerves.

"My mother didn't want me to come today," Jane said.

"Really? Why?"

"The usual. She thought I was favoring my leg too much. I should stay home and rest."

"She's still babying you," I said, hunching over my knees to scrub some mud from my boots. I don't know why I bothered. They would just get dirty at recess.

The ball came near us again. I looked up to see Ole watching me, his gaze curious. I frowned and glanced away.

Jane shrugged a narrow shoulder. "Like always. My leg is fine. I snuck out when her back was turned. I wasn't about to miss a day."

I'd learned soon after starting how seriously Jane took school. She was the most advanced student by far and wanted to be a doctor when she grew up.

Most medical schools refused to educate girls, but Jane told anyone who would listen that wasn't going to stop her. She was already exchanging letters with faculty members at the few schools in Boston and Philadelphia that educated women.

"Aunt Marta couldn't wait for me to get out of the house this morning," I confessed.

"Can you blame her?" Jane asked.

"Ouch," I said. I knew Jane didn't intend to be mean, but her comment still stung. Like everyone else, she thought I was too soft for prairie life.

"I didn't mean to hurt your feelings, Maddy," Jane said, her voice level. "You didn't grow up here. But you'll learn."

"You think so?" I asked.

I wanted to show everyone I wasn't useless. But more than that, I wanted to go home to St. Paul.

Before I could say more, something wet and muddy smacked into my stomach, knocking all the breath from my body. My chest burned and I gasped for air. What had just happened?

# CHAPTER TWO

I hunched over the object that had slammed into my middle. Dazed, I realized a muddy ball had landed in my lap.

"Take a deep breath," Jane instructed me. "Now take another one." She rose to her feet and balanced with one hand against my shoulder, then shouted across the yard. "Hey, you watch yourself, Ole Nilsen!"

I felt my lungs fill. The stars that had clouded my vision began to clear.

Ole jogged over. "It was an accident." He ducked his head, making his hair fall across his eyes.

My heart lurched. I hated that I had a crush on someone who thought so little of me. Especially since it was clear Ole had a crush on Anna.

"Aren't you going to apologize?" Jane demanded.

"Sorry," Ole mumbled. "Can I have the ball back?"

Over his shoulder, I could see Johann and Anna rolling their eyes. I was delaying their game.

Anger flowed through me. I was sick of everyone thinking I was useless.

I heaved myself to my feet and grabbed the ball in both hands. "Here's your stupid ball," I said. Then I flung it with all my might.

In my head, I imagined the ball flying high over Ole's head. It would fly so far it would get lost in the melting snowdrifts. Ole would spend hours trying to track it down.

Instead, the ball slipped out of my grasp.
It landed with a thud at Ole's feet.

Across the yard, Johann and Anna laughed.
Next to me, I heard Jane sigh. Ole just scooped
up the ball, his eyes not meeting mine.

My face burned. So much for proving I wasn't
useless.

Just then, the door to the schoolhouse opened
behind us. We all jumped.

"Why are you blocking the entrance?" Miss
Tyler, the schoolteacher, asked.

"No reason, miss," Jane answered.

Miss Tyler took one look at my muddy dress
and shook her head.

"You can't even keep yourself clean, can you,
Maddy?" she asked, ringing the handbell that
signaled the start of school.

My face burned again. Even our schoolteacher
thought I was too soft. Miss Tyler had grown up on

a farm in Nebraska. Despite being new to town, she understood farm life.

"Sorry, miss," I murmured as I brushed past her.

Everyone else trailed inside too. We left our outerwear and lunch pails in the cloakroom inside the door. I was the only one with a heavy cloak.

"Can't even dress for the weather," Anna muttered. "How pathetic."

Johann snickered.

"Ignore them," Jane reminded me as we walked into the main schoolroom.

I tried, but Anna's words echoed in my head. Would I ever fit in here?

Jane and I took our seats with the other girls on the right side of the room. The boys sat on the left. An enormous potbelly stove—our only source of heat—stood in the middle. Fortunately, the day was warm enough that my hands wouldn't get stiff with cold during lessons.

The morning passed slowly. Elias, Johann's younger brother, and Signe, Anna's younger sister, read aloud from their *McGuffey Readers*. The rest of us worked at our desks.

The sound of chalk on slates filled the room. I did math problems at the desk I shared with Jane and tried to ignore Anna and Ole whispering and giggling behind me.

"Is this right?" I asked, sliding my slate to Jane.

Jane glanced quickly at my work. "Problem three is wrong," she said.

I fixed my mistake, wishing that learning came as easily to me as it did to Jane. She was working on advanced calculus problems from a book she had gotten from one of the medical schools.

A few moments later, Miss Tyler came by to check our work. She sniffed when she saw I had all the problems correct. She pinched her lips together and ignored Jane entirely.

Miss Tyler was only sixteen, just three years older than me. She wasn't a bad teacher, but she had no idea how to do calculus. Instead of encouraging Jane, Miss Tyler chose to pretend she didn't exist. I think Miss Tyler was afraid of not being the smartest person in the room.

Finally, it was time for lunch. We all raced outside, anxious to enjoy more of the unexpected warm weather.

"Does it seem colder than before?" Jane asked as we took our normal spot on the steps.

"Maybe?" I said, opening my lunch pail.

Aunt Marta had packed two slices of bread soaked in molasses. I was glad my lunch hadn't frozen in the cloakroom, like it had for the past few weeks.

"And the sky is different," Jane added.

"I guess," I said, glancing up. The sky had taken on an almost coppery look. "I hadn't noticed."

Jane shook her head. "You need to pay attention to your surroundings out here, Maddy. All the time. No exceptions."

"I know," I grumbled.

Aunt Marta said the same thing to me all the time. I'd never needed to pay attention to my surroundings in St. Paul. My father had always watched out for me. My heart sank as I remembered how alone I was here.

"That's odd," Jane said a minute later.

"What?" I asked, speaking around a mouthful of bread. Jane hadn't touched her lunch yet.

"Those birds are acting strange," she said, pointing to a small apple tree. Several birds hopped from branch to branch.

"Don't birds usually rest in trees?" I asked.

"They usually fly high in good weather," Jane said. "These look like they're waiting for something."

I noticed just then that the yard had grown eerily quiet. The other students had stopped playing and were staring at the sky to the northwest.

"Something's wrong," Jane said.

A chill worked its way down my spine. "Let's go see," I said.

Jane followed me down the steps and to the edge of the building where the others had gathered . . . and then we froze.

"Dear Lord," someone whispered in Norwegian.

I stood, slack-jawed, staring at the sky. The entire northwest horizon was covered with a line of clouds that flashed with silver. It looked as if someone had taken a knife to a featherbed and all the feathers were bursting free.

Instead of feathers, however, it was a swirl of storm clouds—and it was coming our way.

# CHAPTER **THREE**

"Is that lightning?" Anna asked. She squinted at the silvery spikes that shot from the clouds.

I gulped. Even I knew that winter storms didn't normally have lightning.

"This is bad," Johann said, glancing at Ole.

Johann always followed Ole's lead. We all did. As the oldest student, everyone trusted him. Right now, however, Ole looked stunned.

The storm was moving fast, racing toward us across the prairie. A wall of gray clouds swallowed up a line of trees on the horizon. The wind picked up, tearing at our clothing.

Little Elias started to cry. Signe turned and ran back to the schoolhouse door.

"Miss Tyler! Miss Tyler!!" she shouted.

Miss Tyler appeared in the doorway. She frowned at us. "You children should be playing, not standing around idle," she scolded.

She walked down the steps, but as she cleared the edge of the building, a gust of wind hit. Miss Tyler stumbled and stared, her eyes wide with fear.

The sight of our teacher falling to her knees seemed to jolt everyone into action.

"Get back to the school!" Ole bellowed. He yelled something else in Norwegian to Johann, who nodded and went over to Miss Tyler.

I could barely see as Johann helped our teacher to her feet. The wind was so strong that it was hard to stand. Tears streamed down my face.

The edge of the storm was closer now, churning up snow as it raced to engulf us. It looked like someone was pulling a blanket over the prairie. It wasn't a blanket that would keep us warm, however. It was one that would smother us.

Ole scooped up Elias as Anna herded her younger sister into the schoolhouse. I started to follow them when I remembered Jane. She had been right behind me.

I turned in a circle, but I couldn't see her. "Jane!" I screamed.

It was useless. The storm was too loud. The wind carried my voice away.

"Miss Tyler!" I yelled. "Ole! Johann!"

If Jane was out on the prairie, I needed help finding her. I couldn't do it on my own.

At that moment there was a brief pause—the tiniest breath of stillness. It reminded me of my baby cousin when he was about to cry. He would take a tiny inhale right before letting loose. That's what was happening now.

In that stillness, I swore I heard a bird cry from the apple tree at the edge of the yard. I turned in that direction . . . and then the storm hit.

It was like being hit by a train. A mass of ice crystals crawled over every inch of bare skin. The wind was blowing sideways. The world was nothing but a swirling mass of ice.

I held out my hand but couldn't see it. I could barely open my eyes.

I thought of the cloak Aunt Marta had shoved in my hands that morning. How I wished I had it with me now. Bits of ice worked their way down the back of my dress, up my sleeves, and into the tops of my boots.

I had lived through snowstorms before. It snowed a lot in St. Paul every winter. Sometimes the winds would pick up, swirling the snow along the streets. I would watch from the parlor window, safely wrapped in a blanket, a fire crackling on the hearth. I loved watching fat, fluffy snowflakes fall from the sky. Every once in a while, I would stand on the stoop for a few moments. I liked the brief feeling of cold on my cheeks before I went back inside.

This storm was nothing like that. Instead of snow, we had ice. Instead of a warm parlor, I was lost on the prairie. Instead of feeling cozy as I sat before a fire, I worried I might actually die out here.

*Jane. I have to find Jane.*

I wiped the crust of ice from my eyes and opened my mouth to shout. It was a mistake. As soon as I did, ice burned the back of my throat. I coughed, feeling for a moment like I might suffocate.

I turned around and around, trying to get my bearings. I searched in vain for the schoolhouse or the apple tree. I'd even settle for a glimpse of the outhouses. At least then I'd know where I was.

But I couldn't see a single thing except for the ice pellets against my face. Panic rose in my chest, and I began to cry. I couldn't stay here. I had no idea where the school was, so I picked a direction and started walking.

A gust of wind knocked into me. I fell hard, bruising my hip. I was crying freely now, even though the tears were crusting around my eyes. My head spun, and my limbs felt weak.

*They were right,* I thought. *Aunt Marta, Ole, Miss Tyler—even Jane. I am weak. I'm too soft to survive out here. I'm not going to make it.*

# CHAPTER FOUR

I curled up on my side and wrapped my arms around my legs as the snow began to cover me. I pulled my legs closer to my chest, trying to find an ounce of warmth. The wind pummeled me, and I felt certain I was going to die.

Aunt Marta would shake her head when she heard the news.

"I'm surprised she lasted this long," she would say. "It's a shame she wasn't wearing the cloak I gave her."

I cracked an eye, hoping the schoolhouse was visible. All I saw was a swirling mass of ice that pricked my eyeballs.

I closed my eyes again. I was lost, and no one could help me. I just hoped Jane wasn't out here somewhere too.

A tremor shook my body, and I drew a breath, trying to calm my nerves. Then I realized . . . something felt different.

I drew another breath. It took me a moment to grasp what had changed. It was easier to breathe near the ground.

Cautiously, I raised my head. The ice still stung my eyes, but when I held out my hand, I could see my fingertips.

*If I stay near the ground, maybe I can crawl my way to safety,* I thought.

Crawling onto the open prairie was a risk, but if I did nothing, I would freeze to death.

I pushed myself onto my hands and knees and started to move. I had to try.

My breath was ragged in my ears, drowned out only by the wind. It took me a few moments before I heard the sound. It was the handbell that Miss Tyler used to call us to class.

Sobbing, I pulled myself in that direction. The bell got louder and louder.

Suddenly, the school steps loomed before me. Hands grabbed my shoulders and pulled me toward the door. I stumbled on weak legs and fell, exhausted and crying, into the cloakroom.

"Get her as close to the stove as you can," someone commanded. My heart lurched when I recognized Jane's voice.

"Come along, Maddy. You can make it," said Miss Tyler.

She wedged her shoulder beneath my armpit. Another pair of hands supported my other arm.

"Careful," a voice said. I realized it was Ole.

"Thank you," I said. Or at least I tried to say it. My teeth were chattering too hard to make words.

Miss Tyler and Ole eased me down onto the floor.

"We need to dry her out," Jane said, crouching before me. "Maddy? Can you hear me?"

"Yes," I said, laughter and relief flooding through me.

The ice was starting to melt from around my eyes, and my vision was returning. Jane's face was the most beautiful sight I had ever seen.

I glanced over her shoulder and did a quick count of faces. Everyone was there. They were all wrapped in the few scarves and mittens they had brought to school.

"You're all safe!" I exclaimed.

Jane was examining my fingers, bending and extending them. Miss Tyler was unlacing my boots.

Pain shot through my toes as they began to warm and thaw.

"No thanks to you," someone muttered.

Everything stilled for a moment. I glanced around, realizing that no one was smiling. They were all frowning—even the little ones.

"Are you mad at me?" I asked, my voice squeaking.

There was silence. Then Miss Tyler spoke, her voice low. "When the storm hit, everyone else went back to the schoolhouse. You headed in the opposite direction."

"I . . . I thought Jane was on the prairie," I said. "I went to find her."

Jane gave me an appreciative smile. Everyone else still looked angry.

"Well, we've solved one problem," Miss Tyler said, rising to her feet. "Now we need to solve the rest of them."

"What problems?" I asked.

As soon as I asked the question, everyone shook their heads in exasperation. Jane, who was dabbing at my eyes with a damp rag, didn't say anything.

"Ouch, that hurts," I said, flinching as the cloth touched the sensitive skin.

"You rubbed some of the skin off," she said. "It looks like you were coated in ice."

"It's mainly ice out there," I said, pushing to my feet. "Why didn't you put me closer to the fire?"

"The stove is acting funny," Anna said, overhearing my question.

I turned and saw her sitting with the little ones. They were huddled at a corner desk, their bodies pressed against each other. Someone had draped my cloak over them.

"How?" I asked. "It looks normal to me."

"It's been sparking with static electricity. Like how blankets spark at night during the winter,"

Anna explained. "Except these sparks are big. Johann got shocked when he put a log in the fire."

Across the room, Johann held up his hand silently. There was a red mark on his lower arm.

"We're going to have to ration the wood," Miss Tyler said. "I was going to restock the bin from the woodpile after school. I let it get too low."

"Do we have enough for the night?" Jane asked.

Miss Tyler shook her head.

"There should be enough water," Ole said. "I refilled the jug this morning from the well."

Just then, a gust blew through the cracks in the wall. Ice prickled my skin, surprising me. I thought I had left the ice behind, but the blizzard had found a way inside. Snow swirled along the floor and gathered in the corners of the room.

I looked around at the rest of my schoolmates. Their faces were drawn and white. Miss Tyler was clenching her jaw. Ole was pacing back and forth near the windows.

I realized that everyone was scared—terrified. I didn't blame them. It was freezing, and we didn't have enough wood for the stove.

Miss Tyler went to the back of the room. When she turned, I saw she was checking the lunch pails.

"We don't have much food," she said. "Most everyone ate their lunch already."

Signe started to wail. Anna took her sister's hand and murmured a soothing stream of Norwegian in a cheerful voice that sounded fake. Her other hand was balled tightly in her lap.

"Johann and I can go for help," Ole said. "His farm is one mile away. They'll hook up their horses to the wagon and come back to rescue everyone."

"You can't go without me!" Elias called to his brother. But Johann shook his head firmly and shushed him.

Miss Tyler shook her head too. "It's too dangerous. We couldn't even see our hands in front of our faces out there. You'd get lost and freeze to death."

"We won't—" Ole started, but Miss Tyler cut him off.

"We have no choice but to stay," she said. "Everyone, put on your mittens and scarves."

"It won't be enough," Ole argued. He looked determined. "Johann and I can make it to the farm if we follow the road."

"That's only if you find the road," Miss Tyler said. "And then you have to make it back."

"My house is closer," I piped up.

Ole shook his head dismissively. "We'd have to cut cross-country for that," he said. "There aren't enough landmarks."

"It's too dangerous for anyone to leave," Miss Tyler insisted.

Just then a huge gust shook the schoolhouse, rattling all the windows. Someone screamed.

Ole turned back to Miss Tyler. "If we stay here, we'll be trapped," he told her. "We don't have enough food or wood. The storm just started. There's still time for Johann and me to go get help."

Ole and Johann moved to the door, but Miss Tyler was faster. She ran to the cloakroom and plastered herself against the door.

"I forbid you from leaving!" she exclaimed.

"You can't do that, miss," Ole said, tugging mittens onto his hands. Johann wrapped a scarf around his neck.

Inside the schoolroom, we all shifted so we had a view of the door.

"As your teacher, I'm responsible for your safety," Miss Tyler said. "And I'm telling you that you can't leave."

"With all due respect, miss, we're leaving," Ole said. "We'll be back soon with help."

He turned around. His eyes locked with Anna's and then, for a moment, with mine. I stared at him, willing him not to go.

"No! You're staying here!" Miss Tyler shouted.

Then, to everyone's shock, Ole put his hands on Miss Tyler's waist and picked her up. It wasn't hard, since Ole was a good foot taller. He moved our teacher to one side and set her down.

Johann paused. "I'll be back soon. Promise," he said to Elias, who stared at his older brother in disbelief.

Ole shoved the door open. The wind howled, trying to get inside. Then he and Johann were gone.

# CHAPTER FIVE

For a long time, no one said anything. The only sounds were the wind battering the walls and the ice crackling against the windows.

Then Elias started to sob. The sound jolted everyone into action.

Anna quickly organized a game for the little ones. They sat near the stove and rolled a ball back and forth. The entire time, Anna sang a Norwegian folk song I had heard Aunt Marta hum. It seemed to soothe everyone's nerves. Even Elias stopped crying.

Jane started to inventory our supplies, writing a list on her slate.

"Six pairs of mittens, a shovel, three logs of wood," she murmured as she wandered past me.

Miss Tyler searched the shelves in the cloakroom, checking for a lunch pail or scarf she had overlooked earlier.

There didn't seem to be anything for me to do. I sat at one of the desks and stared out the window. It had only been a few hours since lunch and the storm. But it was so dark outside that it looked like night.

I wondered how Ole and Johann were doing. The road was about a hundred feet from the south side of the schoolhouse. If they found it, they would be fine. It ran straight past the Gundersen farm.

I just hoped they found it.

Thinking of the boys trying to get to Johann's cabin made me think of my own family. I was glad

Aunt Marta had kept Cecelia home today. It gave me some comfort to know that my cousin was safe.

*I hope Uncle Hans and the boys were able to get all the cattle back to the barn before the storm hit*, I thought. The blizzard had given me a new appreciation for how tough farm life was.

"Well, that's that," Miss Tyler said, wiping her hands. "We need to ration the wood. And the water."

"I'm hungry," Signe whined.

"Hush," Anna said, gathering the little girl in her lap. Elias had already fallen asleep near the stove underneath my cloak. "Think of how glad our parents will be to know we're safe and sound."

"Okay," the girl said. Her eyes nodded, and soon she was asleep.

"They should be here by now," Jane murmured.

We all knew who she meant. Ever since Ole and Johann had left, I had been listening for the sound of rescue. But there was nothing.

"They'll be here," Miss Tyler said, smiling reassuringly.

"Have you ever been through a storm like this before, miss?" Anna asked.

Miss Tyler shook her head as she sank onto the floor. "We had fierce storms in Nebraska but nothing like this. Although my father did often string a rope from the house to the barn."

"Why?" I asked as everyone else nodded knowledgeably.

Anna's smile was almost friendly. "So you don't get lost and wander onto the prairie during a storm."

"Oh," I said. Memories of my time in the storm came back to haunt me. I had come very close to becoming lost myself.

"We did have locusts one year," Miss Tyler added. "That was awful."

Even I knew about locusts. My dad's newspaper had printed stories about the grasshoppers that descended on the prairie in swarms. They would eat everything in sight—including all the crops that the farmers had so carefully planted.

"We had those a few times too," Jane said. "It was almost like the blizzard."

"How so?" I asked.

"A huge cloud of them would roll across the prairie. You could see them coming but knew you couldn't escape," Jane explained. "Then they'd swarm over everything as they landed. They'd latch onto your clothes. You could hear them chewing."

I shivered. It sounded awful.

"I can't wait to move to the city," Anna declared.

I looked at her in surprise. "You don't want to stay here?" I asked.

Anna made a face. "With all the locusts and droughts and storms? No thank you."

"What do you want to do?" Jane asked.

"I make dresses," Anna said, a little shyly.
"I want to move to St. Paul and open a dress shop."

I smiled encouragingly. "I would buy one of
your dresses."

It was true. Anna's clothes were made of the
same rough, simple fabric as everyone else's.
But her clothes always had precise seams and an
occasional ruffle or bow.

To my surprise, Anna blushed. "What about
you, Maddy?" she asked.

"I . . ." My voice trailed off. "Honestly, I just
want to go back home. I'm no good at farm life."

"Farm life is hard," Anna said as the others
nodded. "Even when things are going well, it's hard.
My parents left Norway because there wasn't any
land left to farm. But this . . ." She looked around
the cold, dark schoolroom. "This is hard."

"You're doing the best you can," Jane said,
taking my hand.

"Thanks," I said. It felt good to be honest about how I was feeling. "I'm sorry I messed up earlier. I should have come back to the school immediately."

Jane, Anna, and Miss Tyler all looked at each other in silence for a moment. Jane was the first to speak.

"You made a mistake. It happens," she said. "We just live in a place where mistakes can be fatal."

Anna nodded. "And it was brave to look for Jane."

"I don't say this enough," Miss Tyler added, "but you're an excellent—"

I never knew how Miss Tyler was going to end that sentence. At that exact moment, there was a huge, deafening crash. In an instant, we were plunged into a swirl of ice.

# CHAPTER SIX

---

Dakota Territory
Inside the schoolhouse
January 12, 1888
3:15 p.m.

---

"What happened?" Jane shouted.

I looked around, confused. Ice stung my face, and a cold wind sliced through my clothes. It felt like being outside. How was that possible?

"The window broke!" Miss Tyler shouted.

I looked over my shoulder. A window had shattered, spilling glass over the floor. Ice and snow rushed inside, swirling through the room.

"The wind did that?" Jane gasped as another gust blew through the opening.

"Hurts!" Signe shouted.

Jane sprang into action, crawling across the floor to the children. I couldn't figure out why she was crawling until I tried to stand. The wind nearly knocked me over.

The children were sobbing. Anna did her best to comfort them as Jane examined their faces. Blood streamed from gashes in their foreheads.

Suddenly Jane gasped and took Anna's hand. Even from across the room I could see a large sliver of glass embedded in the flesh between Anna's thumb and index finger.

"Get everyone to the cloakroom!" Miss Tyler shouted.

Jane helped Anna to her feet. Miss Tyler went to Signe and Elias. I was about to follow when Miss Tyler turned back to me.

"You need to fix the window!" she yelled over the roar of the wind.

I froze, stunned by the terrible power of the storm. The window was smashed. The blizzard outside was monstrous. The six of us were trapped in this tiny schoolhouse. What could I do that would make a difference? There was no hope.

Then I felt a quiet strength settle across my shoulders. *You made it out of the blizzard. You can do this,* I thought to myself.

I staggered to the window, clutching the desks to stay upright. Glass and ice ground beneath my boots.

The window frame was unbroken. If I could find something to nail over the opening, we might be okay.

I looked around frantically. Could I pry off one of the desktops and use that? I clawed at the closest desk, but my hands were so cold they could barely move. The desktop wouldn't budge.

My eyes fell on my cloak, lying discarded on the floor. In the chaos, it must have been forgotten.

I shivered as I forced my way to the cloak. My fingers were so stiff with cold that I dropped the garment twice.

I shook shards of glass from the coat onto the floor, then began the painful walk back to the shattered window. When I finally made it, I held the cloak up to see if it would block the wind.

The blizzard tore through the fabric as if it were made of cobwebs.

A small sob escaped my lips as the cloak fell to the floor. I looked around the room. What else could I use? I thought of the careful list of supplies Jane had been making. A few rough logs and some mittens couldn't help me now.

*You'll have to solve this on your own, Maddy,* I told myself.

I realized I had been staring at Miss Tyler's desk. Unlike the students' desks, hers had drawers. Maybe one of those would work.

I made my way to the desk and pulled out two drawers. A broken slate and a few pieces of chalk clattered to the floor.

Taking a deep breath, I raised the first drawer above my head and brought it down—hard—on the desk. The wood shuddered in my hand, but the drawer didn't break. I tried again, my shoulders aching.

This time, the drawer burst apart. I had done it! We had flat pieces of wood to block the window!

I quickly broke the second drawer apart.

"Tacks!" Miss Tyler shouted from the cloakroom entrance. She inched her way into the room.

"What?" I yelled back.

"Tacks!" she called again. "Top drawer."

I jerked open the top drawer. Five brass tacks and a small hammer rolled around inside. It was the most beautiful sight I had ever seen.

I pocketed the tacks and tucked splintery pieces of wood under my arm. Once we fixed the window, we could bring everyone else back from the cloakroom. The stove would warm us up.

But when I looked at the stove, my insides turned to ice. The fire had gone out.

I felt a flash of panic but steadied my shoulders. I thought of something Aunt Marta often said: "One problem at a time."

She was right. I could only solve one problem at a time. And right now I needed to fix the window.

Miss Tyler met me at the broken window. She held the first piece of wood over the opening.

I fumbled with a tack. It was almost impossible to hold it into place. My fingers were so numb that I dropped it.

"Try another!" Miss Tyler shouted.

I pulled a second tack from my pocket. I lined it up and raised the hammer. I took a swing and

managed to hit the tack, driving it through the wood.

Almost immediately, I knew it was pointless. The tacks were too short to attach to the frame. And the wind was simply too strong. Even if we did manage to get a piece in place, the wind would tear it down.

"Keep trying!" Miss Tyler begged.

I lowered my hands. We couldn't fix the window. It was foolish to spend more energy trying. I drew a deep breath and faced my teacher.

"It won't work!" I said. "I'm sorry."

"It will work," she pleaded, grabbing my hand. "Just try harder!"

I made one more attempt. I sank another tack into the wood from the desk.

Miss Tyler gave a shout of joy. But her face fell when we both let go of the board—it immediately fell to the floor.

Miss Tyler stood in front of the opening and stared at the storm. Another blast of icy air slammed against the schoolhouse.

"We have to go tell the others!" I shouted.

Miss Tyler didn't move.

"We can't fix the window," I said. "There's nothing we can do."

For a second, I thought she was going to argue with me. Tears filled her eyes and spilled down her face. It was strange to see my teacher cry.

"I know," she said, staggering away from the window. Her dress was coated in ice.

We made our way to the cloakroom. Signe sat on Anna's lap. Jane had wrapped a piece of cloth around the gash in Anna's hand. Elias clung to Jane's dress, his eyes wide with fear.

"How is everyone?" I asked.

"No one's bleeding anymore," Jane said. "How's the window?"

"Not good," I said.

I waited for Miss Tyler to tell the others the news, but she just stood next to me crying. It was up to me.

"We don't have anything to fix the window," I said. "We tried everything. The stove has gone out, and the firewood is coated in ice. If we stay here, we'll freeze."

"What are you saying?" Jane asked, looking more afraid than I had ever seen her.

I took a breath and gulped. My words would change everything.

"We need to leave."

# CHAPTER SEVEN

Dakota Territory
Schoolhouse cloakroom
January 12, 1888
3:30 p.m.

"We can't leave," Anna protested. "What about Ole and Johann? They'll get here."

Jane shook her head. "It's been too long."

From behind Jane, Elias peered at me anxiously. No doubt he was worried about his brother.

"I'll bet they're safe," I said, trying to make my voice light. "They probably just decided to wait out the storm at Johann's farm."

"What if they make it back here?" Anna pressed.

"We'll leave a note on the chalkboard explaining that we've gone to my house," I said. "I'll also say that Ole and Johann went to the Gundersen farm, in case someone else comes looking for us."

"Your house?" Jane said.

"It's more than two miles to the Gundersens', even if we find the road." I swallowed, suddenly nervous about presenting my plan. "We go north. Cross-country. Two hundred yards gets us to my house. We'll be safe there."

Jane hesitated, then looked at the children and sighed. I knew she was thinking the same thing I was—they wouldn't make it two miles.

Jane glanced at me. "Can you find your way?"

"Yes," I said. "We head straight up the hill to the cedar. That will point us in the right direction. Then there's an open section."

I glossed over that part, which would be the most dangerous, since there were no landmarks. "After that, we look for the fruit trees."

"Fruit trees?" Anna asked.

"Uncle Hans planted a row of them that leads straight to the house," I explained.

"What do you think?" Jane asked Anna.

"We don't have a choice," she said. "I trust Maddy."

"Really?" I asked. I wasn't sure I even trusted myself.

Jane put a hand on my shoulder. "You've made the right decisions so far. I trust you too."

I felt suddenly terrified. I was responsible for everyone's safety. I swallowed the lump in my throat. I needed to be brave.

Everyone scrambled to put on their warmest clothes. It wasn't much. Everyone had a pair of mittens, at least. Miss Tyler had found two old cloaks, which she draped around Signe and Elias.

An idea occurred to me. "Do we have any rope?" I asked.

"No, why?" Miss Tyler asked.

"We should tie ourselves together," I said. "Like how your father tied a rope to the barn."

"It's not the worst idea," Jane said.

"We could use scarves," Anna suggested.

"Our necks will get cold," Miss Tyler said.

"We'll be cold no matter what," I said. "But I have an idea."

I raced back into the schoolroom and picked up my cloak. Then I went to the chalkboard and scrawled a message on it. That way it was clear we had gone to the Rolvig farm, while Ole and Johann went to the Gundersen farm.

When I got back to the cloakroom, I held out my cloak.

"We can use this to make a rope. Who can tie a good knot?" I asked.

"Let me," Anna said.

Working together, we tore the cloak into long strips. Then Anna took the pieces and tied complicated knots to make one piece. We tied the cloak rope around our waists.

"Hold on and don't let go," I told Signe and Elias.

Since I knew the route, I was at the front of the line. Jane was right behind me, followed by Elias, Anna, and Signe. Miss Tyler took her place at the end of the line.

"Everyone ready?" I asked.

"It will be a fun adventure," Anna sang. We were all trying to be calm for Elias and Signe.

Jane took my hand. Her expression was serious. We both knew what lay outside the door.

"We can do this," she said.

With a bravado I didn't feel, I swung the door open and led us outside. It was much worse than I remembered. The wind howled around us as we stood on the steps.

I couldn't believe Jane and I had sat there hours earlier, enjoying the warm weather. The world had been completely transformed. Now it was a swirling gray mass of deadly snow and ice.

"Let's go!" I tried to say, but ice filled my mouth. I bent at the waist and coughed.

Jane bumped into me, and I stumbled a little. I grabbed the railing as my foot sank into a drift. Immediately, snow filled my boot.

*Well, you can't stay here,* I told myself. There was no choice but to find the cedar at the top of the hill.

I turned left at the bottom of the stairs. The snow was drifting heavily around our feet. It was up to my knees in some spots.

*Signe and Elias must be sinking up to their waists,* I realized.

I had hoped we could sink beneath the storm and crawl for a bit, like I had before, but that would be impossible. The snow was too deep.

Around us, the storm was like a living, breathing monster. It flew at us, hurling ice against our faces.

It tore at our clothes and howled in our ears. Icy shards crept up our sleeves and down our necks. We would be living ice sculptures if we didn't make it to my farm.

Walking was difficult. Every time I took a step, the cloak rope tightened at my waist. I had to wait for the others to catch up before I could take the next step.

"We need to walk faster!" I shouted at Jane.

She was directly behind me, but I could barely make out her shape. I had to yell directly into her ear. I felt Jane nod and heard her shout the directions to Elias.

I pressed forward, feeling the ground rise beneath my feet. We were on the hillside, at least. Our pace picked up slightly.

I heard muffled shouts behind me. In the moment the wind paused, I realized it was Anna. She was calling out a walking rhythm.

"Step! Step! Step! Good job!" she shouted.

I thought about Ole and Johann. Had they managed to stay together? Had they made it to Johann's farm?

*Of course they did*, I told myself. They were both strong and had good heads on their shoulders. They would know it was too dangerous to come back to us. We would see them tomorrow. I had to believe that.

By the time we made it to the top of the rise, my lungs burned. I stopped suddenly, trying to get my bearings. *Where is the tree?*

Jane crashed into me, and I staggered a bit. Jane grabbed my elbow before I fell.

"Do you see the tree?" I yelled into her ear.

"What?"

"The tree? Do you see it?" I shouted.

Jane turned around, the cloak pulling at my waist.

"Tree!" I heard her shout. Anna shouted something in reply, but I couldn't make out what it was.

The tips of my ears were burning, like I had fallen asleep against a stove. The skin around my eyes was coated in ice. I rubbed at it, wincing as the ice tore the scabs that had formed earlier.

I didn't have time to worry about my ears or eyes right now. We needed to find the tree. If we didn't, we risked wandering onto the open prairie. If that happened, we wouldn't make it.

"We can't see it!" I heard Anna shout back to Jane.

"Maddy! We're lost!" Jane yelled at me.

Tears squeezed out of my eyes, stinging the raw skin. I had failed. I had gotten us lost on the prairie. We were going to die, and it was all my fault.

# CHAPTER EIGHT

Dakota Territory
Top of the hill
January 12, 1888
3:55 p.m.

I knew I needed to stay still and observe the
landscape. If we were lucky, the wind would die
down briefly and we might see the tree.

I made it two steps before something smacked
me across the face. I fell to the ground. Jane landed
next to me.

"Are you okay?" Jane asked.

"Maybe," I gasped.

I wiped the snow from my eyes. Pain shot
through my right hip, which had taken the brunt
of my fall. I groaned and rolled to my side.

Suddenly I realized something—I could hear Jane. We were both speaking in our normal voices. We didn't have to shout to be heard. The wind had died down, and ice wasn't pelting my face.

"What—" I started to ask.

"Look up," Jane said.

I raised my eyes and gasped. The branches of the cedar tree arched overhead, creating a small shelter. Everyone else had crammed their way into the spot. Signe and Elias were pressed against Anna. Miss Tyler rubbed her hands together. Everyone wore the same expression—hope.

"We made it to the tree," I said. Tears of relief poured down my face.

"Don't cry or it will freeze," Miss Tyler warned.

"You're right," I said, dabbing at my face. My mittens were frozen, and the ice scraped my skin.

"Now comes the hard part," Anna said. She reached down to haul Jane and me to our feet.

I knew she was right. The worst part of the journey was ahead of us. There were no landmarks between the tree and the farm. Nothing we could use to navigate our way to safety. No buildings, no fences, not even a giant rock or two. Just the prairie stretching for miles in all directions.

We would have to rely on sheer luck and prayers. Otherwise we would wander onto the open prairie and freeze to death.

Signe tugged my sleeve. "Can't we stay here?"

A blast of cold air shook the tree. Snow from the upper branches fell on us. It was tempting to camp under the tree, but it would be foolish.

"We can't stay here," Jane announced. "It keeps getting colder."

Signe looked like she was about to cry.

"Wouldn't you rather be nice and warm by the fire?" Anna said. "With warm socks and dry feet?"

Signe responded with a serious nod.

"I can't feel my fingers," Elias complained, holding up his bare hands. His fingers were as pale as marble.

"Put your mittens back on!" Anna commanded. She took Elias's mittened hands between her own and started to rub them briskly.

"Frostbite," Jane whispered to me.

Everyone on the prairie knew the dangers of frostbite. If the temperature was cold enough, skin could freeze. If it didn't warm up in time, the frozen parts needed to be amputated.

I thought back to the stories I'd heard of people who had lost fingers or toes. I tried flexing my own fingers, but I couldn't really bend them.

Anna met my eyes over the little ones' heads. "We need to keep moving."

I nodded, bracing myself for what was to come.

"In one minute, we're going to walk onto the prairie," I told the group. "We will walk in as straight a line as possible. There is a fence to the right of the cabin. There's a line of fruit trees to the left. We go together, and we don't let go of the rope. Understand?"

Everyone nodded. I felt like one of the military generals I had read about in my history book. I wondered if everyone else was as frightened as I was right now.

Moving slowly, we made our way around the tree to the spot that faced the farm. Then there was no choice but to step into the storm.

As soon as we left the tree's shelter, snow and ice engulfed us. The wind whipped through my dress, and I shivered uncontrollably. The storm clawed at us, trying to drag us to the ground.

I refused to fall. I took one step, then another. Snow poured into my boots. I couldn't feel my toes.

*Will they have to amputate them? Will I lose my fingers? Will any of us survive this storm?*

Worries threatened to overwhelm me, but I knew I had to stay focused. It would take only a few wrong steps to take us off course.

We kept moving. It was impossible to know how long we walked. I felt the tug and drag of the rope around my waist. Sometimes I thought I heard Jane behind me, muttering under her breath, or Anna singing hymns. But it was probably a trick of the wind.

A strong tug on the rope brought me up short. Jane grabbed my arm and tried to shout something in my ear. It took a long time to figure out what Jane was trying to say.

"Miss Tyler! Glove!"

Jane's face was a blur in the snow swirling between us. She kept pointing behind her.

"What's happening?" I shouted.

Jane leaned over to yell in my ear. "Miss Tyler lost a mitten. She's trying to go back for it!"

"What?" I exclaimed. "She can't do that. She'll get us all lost!"

"She won't listen to Anna!" Jane shouted. "You have to go talk to her."

Frustration welled up within me. We didn't have time for this. I couldn't reach Miss Tyler unless I dragged Jane with me. We risked getting turned around completely.

A plan bubbled up in my head. "Follow me," I said to Jane.

We doubled back to where Anna stood. Her pale eyelashes were crusted with frost.

"Keep facing forward," I told Anna. "Don't look back at us. You need to keep us pointed in the right direction."

Anna nodded.

When I reached Miss Tyler, she was fumbling with the knot at her waist. One hand was tucked into a maroon mitten. The other was bare.

"Miss Tyler!" I shouted. My voice was raw from yelling over the wind.

"I have to go back for my mitten!" she shouted.

I was close enough to see my teacher's frightened face. "We have to leave it," I said.

"No. My mother made it for me. I can't lose it," she insisted, trying to untie the rope.

At that moment, I felt a wave of compassion. Miss Tyler was as scared as the rest of us. I put my hands on hers. Her fingers stilled. Even over the storm, I could hear her sob.

"It's going to be okay," I said. "We just need to stay calm and take it one step at a time."

Miss Tyler was shaking her head. "It's too hard. I'm scared."

"I'm scared too," I said. "But we have to keep going. No matter what."

I wasn't sure if the wind stole my words or not. But Miss Tyler stopped fidgeting and nodded.

I made my way back along the line.

"I haven't moved," Anna told me. "But we need to hurry. The little ones aren't doing well."

I glanced at where Elias and Signe were half collapsed against Anna's legs. "Just a little farther," I said.

I took a step, feeling everyone fall into line behind me. I took another step and then a third. After a hundred steps, I stopped counting. Panic gripped my throat.

*Where is the fence? Where is the farm?*

Out of nowhere, a sudden gust of wind plowed into us. I don't know who stumbled first, but we all went down like dominoes.

I started to shake and push myself to my feet, but my legs wouldn't obey. Instead, I lay in a heap on the frozen ground as ice pelted my face and tried to accept the truth—we were lost.

# CHAPTER **NINE**

Dakota Territory
Open prairie
January 12, 1888
4:35 p.m.

Tears coursed down my face. I had failed.
I had gotten us all lost. Now we were going to die.

*Everyone was right all along*, I thought. *I'm not cut out for prairie life.*

"Jane?" I whispered.

The wind howled so loudly that I couldn't hear my own voice. There was no movement behind me. Had everyone else given up too?

I dropped my head back on the snow. My body was shivering so hard that I couldn't control it. I told myself to get up. I had to get everyone else up too. But it seemed too hard. Instead, I closed my eyes.

In my mind, I wandered down a long corridor, passing open doors. My father's face peeked out of one, smiling sadly. I saw my cousins standing near another and my schoolmates at a third.

At the end of the hallway, I saw a young woman with dark eyes. I recognized her from a photo on the mantle in my old home. It was my mother.

*I must be dying, and my mother has come to get me,* I thought groggily.

The woman opened her mouth, but the voice that came out belonged to Aunt Marta. "Maddy, get up," she said.

My mother blurred and turned into Aunt Marta. "You need to get up," she said. "Keep going. Don't give up."

"Too tired," I murmured. "I failed."

"Nonsense. You'll only fail if you don't get up."

I woke with a start and rolled onto my side. Jane lay with her back to me.

My dream rushed into my mind, followed by a singular thought. *I have to save Jane and the others.*

I reached out a hand and poked Jane repeatedly. "We need to get up," I said when she finally stirred.

Jane groaned and raised her head. "Are we close?"

Truthfully, I had no idea how far we were from the farm. If we were lucky, we might find a hay bale where we could spend the night.

"We can't stay here," I said, dodging the question. "We're going to have to—"

At that moment, the snow lifted briefly. The wall of gray parted, and I saw the row of scraggly fruit trees that my uncle had planted. They were only ten yards away.

"Jane! Fruit trees!" I shouted, stumbling to my feet. "Did you see?"

"You did it!" Jane yelled. "We're saved!"

Our shouting had a ripple effect on the others. The rope around my waist tightened and relaxed while everyone else stood up.

"We're going to make it!" Anna shouted. Tears streamed down her face.

We stumbled to the line of trees, flinging ourselves at the trunks. Just then, I heard a noise. It sounded like a plate being dropped on the floor over and over again.

"This way!" I bellowed, tugging on the rope.

We crept slowly from tree to tree. The wind howled around us, unwilling to let us go. After a few minutes, the sound stopped.

"Everyone, start shouting!" I yelled.

Behind me, my classmates and teacher started whooping and hollering. Over the din, I heard the thudding sound start again.

A few steps farther, and we collided with the cabin. We clung to the side of the structure as we inched our way toward the doorway. The noise got louder and louder.

Suddenly, Aunt Marta materialized out of the storm. She was standing in the doorway, banging a wooden spoon against a pan. When she caught sight of us, her eyes widened with shock.

"You're safe!" she exclaimed. She flung her arms around my neck.

Our hug didn't last long. Everyone was eager to get inside. They surged forward, and we all fell into the cabin. I was overjoyed to see that Uncle Hans and all my cousins were safely inside.

For the next several minutes, Aunt Marta oversaw a flurry of activity. She got us all to the stove and ordered us to unwrap our outerwear. Jane changed the bandage on Anna's hand, then checked everyone's fingers and toes. Signe's pinky finger was an unhealthy shade of white, as were several of Miss Tyler's toes.

My hands were shaking so badly that I couldn't undo the cloak rope. Soft hands brushed my fingers to the side. I looked in surprise as my cousin Cecelia tended to the knots.

"I'm glad you're safe," she whispered.

"Thanks," I said. "I'm glad you stayed home today."

Cecelia's eyes darted over to Elias and Signe. Aunt Marta was wrapping them in a blanket.

"I know," Cecelia said. Then she looked up at me. "You were brave."

I shook my head. "I wasn't bra—"

"You were, Maddy," Miss Tyler interrupted, drawing everyone's attention. "Maddy kept her head and led us to safety. We wanted to stay in the schoolhouse, but a window broke. Maddy was the first to recognize that we needed to leave. And she used every tool available to keep us safe on the prairie. If it weren't for her, we'd be lost."

All eyes turned on me. I shifted uncomfortably in my seat. I didn't like to be the center of attention.

"I was so scared," I admitted. "And I almost gave up."

"But you got up again," Jane said. "And you got us up too."

"Good girl," Aunt Marta said.

I blushed. It was the best compliment I had ever received.

Aunt Marta shoved a cup of hot soup into my hands. I was almost too exhausted to sip it. I drifted a little as the others exchanged stories.

Uncle Hans and the boys had been tending the cattle when the storm hit. They'd managed to get most of the cattle to the barn, only to discover the barn door snowed shut. After clearing the snow, they'd gotten all the cattle inside but had almost lost their way back to the house. Aunt Marta had banged on a pot to guide them.

"That's what gave me the idea to bang on a pot at the front door," Aunt Marta explained. "We hoped you were able to stay at the schoolhouse, but in case you hadn't, we knew we were the closest farm."

Elias made a little sobbing noise. I realized he was probably thinking about his brother Johann. We were all worried that he and Ole hadn't made it to the Gundersen farm.

Anna pulled her arm around him and tucked him close. "They'll be fine," she murmured, although her eyes looked worried.

"Well, no use worrying about what we can't control," Aunt Marta said, rubbing her hands together briskly. "We could all use a good night's sleep."

Within minutes, the front room had been turned into a blanket fort. Everyone hunkered down close to the stove.

My eyelids started drooping. Before I knew it, someone was tucking me into bed.

The wind howled around the cabin, clawing like it was trying to get inside. But even that didn't bother me. Safe and warm, I fell into a dreamless sleep.

---

Dakota Territory
Rolvig cabin
January 13, 1888
8:00 a.m.

---

It felt like only minutes had gone by when I opened my eyes. Sunlight streamed through the window, and an eerie silence filled the room.

I raised my head and met Jane's eyes. "What's different?" I asked. "It's so quiet."

"The storm is over," Jane replied. "It blew itself out before dawn."

I drew in a deep breath. "It's over," I said. "We made it."

Jane squeezed my hand. "We made it."

Anna's family arrived first that morning. They had gone to the school at first light, but my note had directed them to us. Anna's parents cried as they hugged their daughters.

Jane's family came next. Jane's mother fell to her knees, sobbing in relief. She then fussed over Jane, worrying about her daughter's leg, until Jane settled her into a chair with a cup of coffee.

"My leg is fine," Jane said. "It carried me across the prairie during a blizzard, after all. I'm stronger than you think."

"You're right," Jane's mother said. "You're all incredibly strong."

I felt warmth flow through me. I was stronger than I'd thought. The storm had taught me that.

The warmth fled as soon as the next visitors arrived. Elias and Johann's father arrived, his shoulders relaxing when he saw Elias.

"I came from the schoolhouse," Mr. Gundersen said, scooping Elias up in a hug. He scanned the room over his son's head and his face fell. "Johann?" he whispered. "And . . . and Ole?"

Elias stiffened in his father's embrace. "Johann went home, Papa," he said. "He and Ole went home to get help, but we had to leave. The window broke."

"I tried to stop them," Miss Tyler said. Her face was ashen.

"Papa, Johann went home. Let's go find him," Elias urged. He pounded his little fists on his father's shoulders.

Tears were leaking from Mr. Gundersen's eyes. "I saw the note you left," he said. "I hoped it was a mistake. I prayed they came here instead."

"Peter, what are you saying?" Aunt Marta asked.

Mr. Gundersen's voice cracked. "Ole and Johann didn't make it home. I have no idea where they are."

# CHAPTER TEN

Dakota Territory
Rolvig cabin
January 13, 1888
10:30 a.m.

Uncle Hans and his sons left immediately to join the search. Anna and Jane's fathers went with them, leaving the rest of their families with us.

The temperature had plummeted even further overnight, which I hadn't thought possible. It was so cold, we could see our breath indoors. Jane, Anna, and I all huddled in a circle near the stove.

"Are Signe and Miss Tyler going to be okay?" I asked. I glanced toward the small bedroom where they were both asleep.

"Signe's finger looks like it's recovering," Jane said. "I'm worried that Miss Tyler might lose a few toes, though. They should both see the doctor soon."

"Losing a finger or toe would be awful," I said.

"Honestly, if that's the case, they'd be one of the luckier ones," Jane said.

She was right. Over the past few hours, several neighbors had visited to check on us and bring news.

The Larsens had lost track of all their cattle in the storm. The animals had frozen to death.

Nels Andersen had gotten caught on his way back from town. Neighbors had found him huddled in the shelter of his wagon. He was still alive, but when he stood up, he immediately keeled over and died.

Lena Olsen was doing chores when the storm hit. She spent the night in a haystack but would probably lose both feet to frostbite.

"What . . . what do you think about Ole and Johann's chances?" I could barely get the words out.

Anna buried her face in her hands, but Jane met my gaze evenly.

"They're young and strong," she said. "We can hope for the best, but it's a serious situation."

I dabbed at my eye with the corner of a blanket. "We shouldn't have let them go," I said quietly.

"None of us could have held them back," Anna said. She wiped tears from her face. "They thought they were doing the right thing. Just like we did."

"Pancakes are ready," Aunt Marta interrupted. She and Cecelia had been busy making breakfast.

We ate in silence, all of us lost in our own thoughts. Waiting for news was terrible. All our attention was focused on the door, looking for Uncle Hans to return—hopefully with good news.

I helped Cecelia clean up as Aunt Marta left to check on the cows. Uncle Hans and the boys returned just as Aunt Marta came back from the barn.

As soon as I saw his face, I knew there was something worse than waiting.

Uncle Hans shook his head as he unwrapped his scarf. Anna started crying immediately. So did Cecelia.

"They must have gotten lost in the storm," he said slowly. "We found them two miles south of the school, huddled together in a ravine."

"They died?" I asked, my voice a squeak.

"Yes," Uncle Hans said.

Images of Ole's curious face and Johann's serious one danced through my head. I would never see those faces again. They would never grow up, never become farmers or teachers or explore any of their dreams. They would never get married or run off to the city. Just like that, their lives were finished, cut short by a freak storm.

There was nothing left to do or say. I buried my face in my hands and cried.

It was almost two weeks before I returned to school. Miss Tyler had lost three toes to frostbite and had gone back to Nebraska to recover. We would have a new teacher soon, but for now, Jane was leading lessons.

"You're afraid," Aunt Marta said when I resisted returning. The blizzard hadn't changed her bluntness.

"I'm not afraid," I said, looking up from the dough I was kneading. My baking had gotten much better. The bread I made was almost edible now.

"You're afraid of walking across the prairie again," she said.

I dropped my head. Aunt Marta put her hand on my shoulder.

"It's normal to feel afraid," she said.

I looked up at her in surprise. "Really?" I asked.

Aunt Marta let out a rusty laugh. "You expected me to tell you that fear made you weak."

"You always point out how useless I am," I said. "I thought my fear made me useless too."

My aunt's eyes fluttered shut. "I have been too hard on you. When you first came to us, you were not used to prairie life. It's dangerous out here. It's my responsibility to keep you safe."

I held still, not wanting to interrupt.

"You are strong," she continued. "Very strong. I'm proud of how you saved your friends. So is your father," she added.

My hand reached for the letter in my pocket. It had arrived a few days ago. Aunt Marta had written to my father soon after the storm. He had replied right away, telling me how relieved he was that I was safe and how proud he was of me.

"I was so scared," I admitted.

"Of course you were," Aunt Marta said. "I would have been afraid in your shoes. But you didn't let that stop you. You didn't let fear keep you from taking the first step. Don't let it stop you now."

---

Dakota Territory
Rolvig farmyard
January 26, 1888
8:30 a.m.

---

The next day, I stood on the edge of the farmyard. The wind was cold but not biting. Sun glinted off the snow.

Uncle Hans had fixed the broken window in the schoolhouse a few days ago. His tracks led the way across the prairie. Up ahead, I could see the cedar tree that had sheltered and guided us during the storm. The schoolhouse was waiting on the other side. So were Jane and Anna.

I remembered Aunt Marta's words. "You can do this," I told myself under my breath.

I took the first step, my boots crunching on the snow. Then I took another and another.

Moving slowly, I made my way across the prairie, remembering the fear and confusion I had felt during the blizzard. It had been awful, but we had made it—not because we were better or stronger than those who hadn't. It wouldn't have taken much for us to go off course, just like Ole and Johann.

Before I knew it, I was at the cedar tree. I looked down at the schoolhouse. Anna and Jane sat on the steps, talking. When they saw me, they jumped up and waved. I raised my hand, returned the wave, and went down to join my friends.

I didn't know why things had worked out the way they had. There didn't seem to be much rhyme or reason to it. But I was thankful we had lived, even as I would always mourn those who had died. Life was precious, and I would make the most of it.

# A NOTE FROM THE AUTHOR

I grew up in Wisconsin, a state known for its harsh winters. When I was a kid, I loved snowstorms. They were an excuse to make popcorn, watch movies, and drink hot chocolate. It didn't matter what the weather was like outside. We were safe and warm inside.

I never lived through a storm quite like the blizzard of 1888. I did, however, live through the Halloween blizzard of 1991, a storm so big it has its own Wikipedia page! Whenever the anniversary approaches, my friends and I dust off our tales of the storm. Telling stories is how we make sense of momentous events.

The survivors of the 1888 blizzard told stories too. Those stories lived on in newspaper accounts and family legends. They have been collected in books like *The Children's Blizzard* by David Laskin and *The Blizzard Voices* by Ted Kooser.

I drew on many of those stories when writing about Maddy's experiences. There are stories of women banging on pots and pans to lead their husbands and children safely from the barn to the house. Stories of settlers caught driving home in the storm and forced to shelter overnight in their wagons. Stories of cattle that died when their faces froze to the ground. Stories of schoolteachers who led their students across open prairies, forced to take shelter in haystacks.

There is even one story of a brave teacher in Nebraska named Minnie Freeman, who tied a rope around her students' waists so they didn't get separated. Although the story has been disputed, all of Minnie's students made it to safety.

The blizzard Maddy survived impacted huge portions of the American Plains. On January 12, 1888, it hurtled across Montana before blasting the Dakota Territory (now North and South Dakota), Nebraska, Kansas, Minnesota, and parts of Iowa. The storm hit the Dakota Territory and Nebraska in late morning or early afternoon. The weather leading up to the storm had been unexpectedly warm, and many people were taking advantage by doing outdoor chores.

The blizzard is often called the Schoolhouse Blizzard or Children's Blizzard because of the number of students who were trapped at school when it hit. Like

Maddy and her friends, those students had a choice to make. They had to decide if they stood a better chance of surviving if they sheltered in the freezing schoolhouses or braved the prairie. Although it was safer to stay in the schoolhouse, if possible, there weren't any truly good choices in these situations.

Historians think anywhere from 250 to 500 people died in the storm, although the exact number is difficult to estimate. Not every death was recorded and, sadly, not every body was found immediately. Some of the dead were not discovered until months later, when the snow melted. Many other survivors had to have fingers, toes, or even parts of their legs amputated due to frostbite.

Even beyond the blizzard, prairie life was difficult. Settlers experienced hardships such as droughts, locusts, and disease. Like Aunt Marta and Uncle Hans, settlers arrived from Norway and other European countries, looking for a better life. We should not forget, however, that the land these immigrants settled on did not belong to them. The United States government broke treaties and stole land from the people who made up the Oceti Sakowin, sometimes known as the Sioux Nation. Few accounts are available about how these nations survived the blizzard. As a result, their experiences are not included in this book. This reminds us, however, of the need to seek out and tell everyone's stories as best we can.

At the start of this story, Maddy thinks she isn't strong enough for prairie life. She believes she is lacking the outer toughness needed to survive. By the end, however, Maddy learns that real strength comes from within—from being brave enough to show up. Her friends teach her to dream big and make plans to help those dreams come true. Through their deaths, Ole and Johann teach Maddy to make the most of her life.

I don't know if Maddy stays with Aunt Marta or goes to live with her father again, once he gets settled. I do know, however, that no matter what Maddy does, she will never again doubt her own abilities and strength. She will certainly feel fear again, but she will not let fear keep her from taking that first step.

Dreaming big is such an important part of life. Fear is also natural. I hope that you make time in your life to identify your dreams and remember that bravery comes from acting even when we are afraid.

# MAKING CONNECTIONS

1. At first, Maddy feels like she doesn't fit in with her classmates or with prairie life in general. But she later bonds with her classmates, learning about their hopes and dreams. When you find yourself in a new and unfamiliar situation, what are some things you do to make yourself feel more comfortable?

2. After the blizzard hits, Miss Tyler and the students have to make a difficult decision—should they stay or go? If you didn't know the outcomes for the characters, what decision would you have made in that situation, and why?

3. As Aunt Marta teaches Maddy, being brave isn't necessarily the same as being fearless. Think about a time in your life when you had to be brave. What were the circumstances? How did you deal with any feelings of fear or uncertainty? Then look back through this story. Find three times Maddy had to make a decision and show bravery.

# GLOSSARY

**amputate** (AM-pyuh-tayt)—to cut off someone's arm, leg, or other body part, usually because the part is damaged

**atlas** (AT-luhs)—a book of maps

**bravado** (bruh-VAH-doh)—confident or brave talk or behavior that is intended to impress other people

**chaos** (KAY-os)—total confusion

**criticism** (KRI-tuh-si-zuhm)—pointing out the strengths and weaknesses of others

**drought** (DROUT)—a long period of weather with little or no rainfall

**efficient** (uh-FI-shuhnt)—not wasteful of time or energy

**faculty** (FAK-uhl-tee)—the entire teaching staff of a school

**fatal** (FEY-tuhl)—causing death

**frostbite** (FRAWST-byt)—a condition that occurs when cold temperatures freeze skin

**horizon** (huh-RYE-zuhn)—the line where the sky and land seem to meet

**inventory** (IN-vuhn-tor-ee)—to make a complete list of something

**locust** (LOH-kuhst)—a type of grasshopper that flies in huge swarms and eats and destroys crops

**McGuffey Readers** (muh-GUHF-ee REE-duhrs)—a series of textbooks for grades one to six used in American schools in the mid-nineteenth to early twentieth centuries

**numb** (NUM)—unable to feel anything, especially because of cold

**parlor** (PAHR-lur)—a formal living room

**prairie** (PRAIR-ee)—a large area of flat or rolling grassland with few or no trees

**precise** (pri-SISE)—very accurate or exact

**ration** (RASH-uhn)—to limit to prevent running out of something

**ravine** (ruh-VEEN)—a deep, narrow valley with steep sides

**slate** (SLAYT)—a very hard, thin piece of rock in a wooden frame that was used in schools in the past for writing on with chalk

**swarm** (SWORM)—a very large number of insects moving together

photo credit: Sarah Byrnes

## ABOUT THE AUTHOR

Julie Gilbert has been writing and publishing since the fourth grade, when she stapled together a series of graphic novels about her cat. Julie is the author of the Dark Waters series from Stone Arch Books, as well as several titles in the Girls Survive series. She also has written *Cemetery Songs*, a novel for young adults. Julie's novels consider themes of identity and belonging, often with a healthy dose of fantasy and magic. She lives with her family in Minnesota.

photo credit: Wendy Tan

## ABOUT THE ILLUSTRATOR

Wendy Tan is a Chinese-Malaysian illustrator based in Kuala Lumpur, Malaysia. Over the past few years, she has contributed to numerous animation productions and advertisements. Now Wendy's passion for storytelling has led her down a new path: children's book illustration. When she's not drawing, Wendy likes to spend time playing with her mixed-breed rescue dog, Lucky.